What a Funny Bunny

ABC Adventures

Written by Pat Whitehead

Illustrated by Don Page

Troll Associates

Library of Congress Cataloging in Publication Data

Whitehead, Patricia.
    What a funny bunny.

    (ABC adventures)
    Summary: A clumsy Easter Bunny keeps losing the eggs
and candy he is carrying in his basket. A letter of the
alphabet appears on each page accompanied by an appro-
priate word from the text.
    1. Children's stories, American. [1. Rabbits—Fiction.
2. Easter—Fiction. 3. Alphabet] I. Page, Don, ill.
II. Title. III. Series.
PZ7.W5852Wh   1985   [E]   84-8833
ISBN 0-8167-0361-2 (lib. bdg.)
ISBN 0-8167-0362-0 (pbk.)

Aa

It is Easter morning.
Achoo! Crash! Bang! Smash!
There has been an accident!

Bb

Bunny

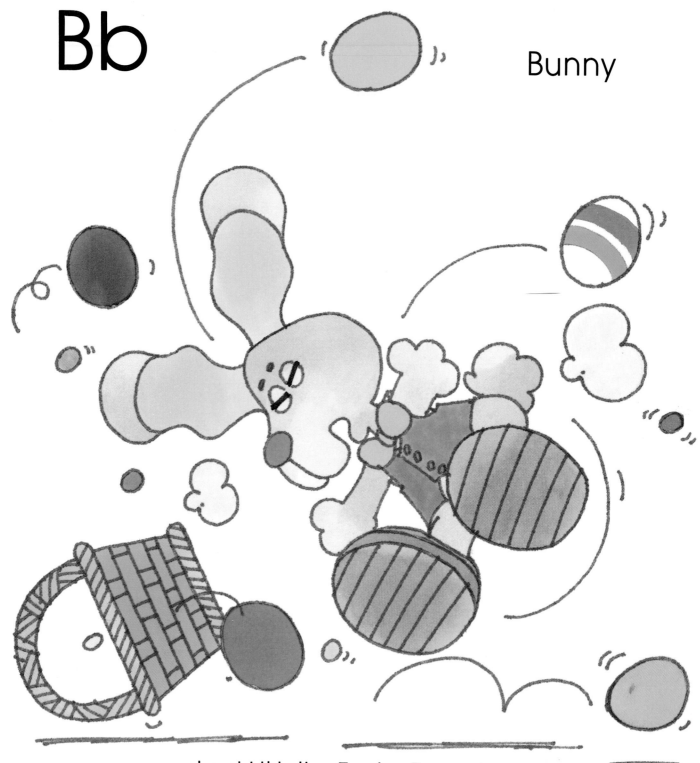

Look! It is the Easter Bunny!

Cc

clumsy

What a clumsy bunny!

Dd

dropped

He dropped his basket.

Ee

eggs

Where are the Easter eggs?
Does anybody know?

Ff

flowers

Some are in the flowers.

Gg

grass

Some are on the grass.

Hh

hedges

And some are between the hedges.

Ii

is

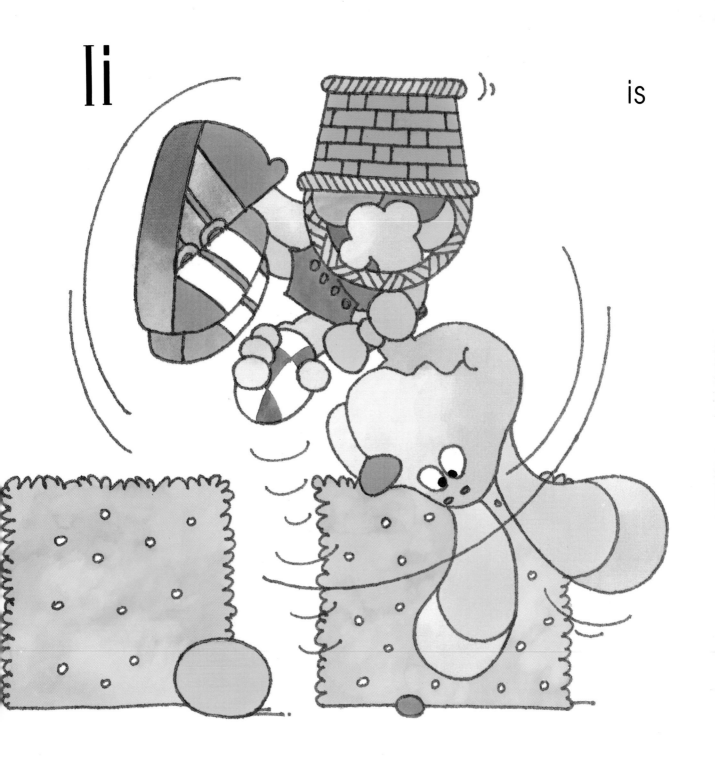

He certainly is a clumsy bunny.

Jj

jellybeans

Where are the jellybeans?
Does anybody know?

Kk

kitten

The kitten knows.

Ll

lamb

The lamb knows.

Mm

mouse

And the tiny gray mouse knows.

Nn

Nibble

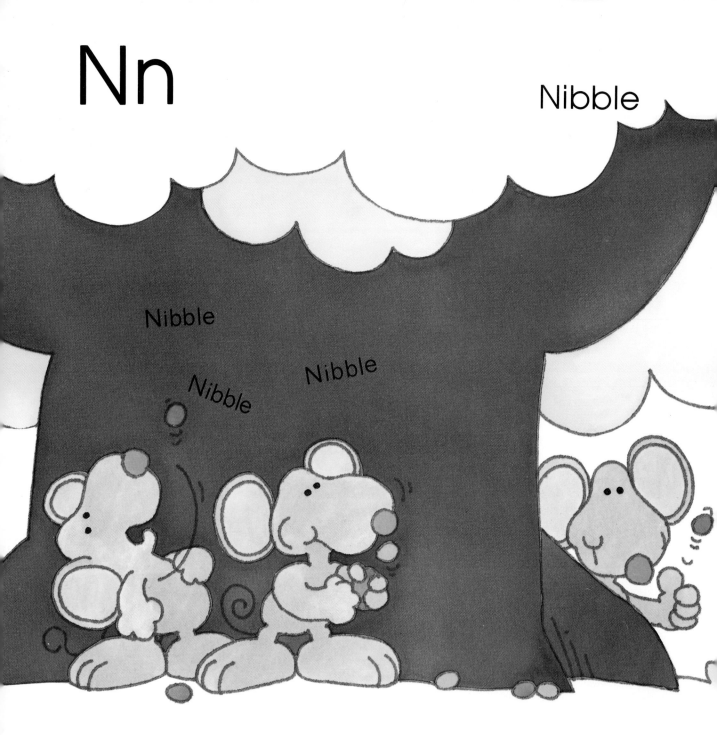

Nibble, nibble, nibble.
They are nibbling the jellybeans.

Oo

Oh

"Oh no!" says the bunny.
"There won't be any left."

Pp

Please

"Please don't eat my jellybeans."

Qq

Quit

"Quit it! Stop at once!"

Rr

rabbits

Now where are my chocolate rabbits?
Does anybody know?

Ss

strawberry

They are not in the strawberry patch.

Tt

toadstools

They are not near the toadstools.

Uu

under

And they are not under the bushes.

Vv

vest

"I remember," says the Easter Bunny.
"They are in my vest. They are safe
inside my vest."

Ww

whiskers

His whiskers wiggle happily.

Xx

Excuse

"Excuse me, excuse me, Easter Bunny,"
calls the mouse as he runs by.
Achoo! Crash! Bang! Smash!

Yy

Yuck

"Yuck," says the Easter Bunny.
"What a mess."

Zz

zoom

"Now I'll have to zoom home for more."

"What a funny bunny I am!"

HAPPY EASTER!